Officer Jack

UNDERWATER

To: Miss Kate
Be Brave!

By **JAMES BURD BREWSTER**

Illustrated by **MARY BARROWS**

J2B PUBLISHING

Published By J2B Publishing LLC, Pomfret, MD

J2B Publishing LLC
4251 Columbia Park Road
Pomfret, MD 20675

This book is set in Garamond. Designed by Mary Barrows

ISBN:
978-1- 941927-39- 7 Paperback
978-1- 941927-40- 3 Hard Cover

Visit www.GladToDoIt.net

Acknowledgement:

This Officer Jack episode is based upon a real response conducted by Auckland, New Zealand police officers, Paul Watts and Simon Russell, on February 17, 2015, who rescued a woman from her sinking automobile by smashing out the rear windshield with a big rock and pulling her through the hole. Within 40 seconds of rescuing the woman, her car disappeared completely underwater. When asked about the rescue, both officer's responded, "It's just another day on the job."

Dedication:

This book is dedicated to police officers everywhere (Federal, State, County, and City) who daily place themselves in harm's way in order to save lives, protect property, and preserve public safety.

Officer Jack and Officer Kate were on foot patrol in Riverfront Park.

"This is one of the prettiest places in Hamilton Township," said Officer Kate.

"Sure is," replied Officer Jack. "I canoe here once a month. I use the boat ramp."

"Help! Help! Someone Help!"

"That came from the boat ramp," said Officer Jack. "Let's go!"

Officer Jack and Officer Kate ran toward the ramp. People on the river bank were pointing into the water.

"Over here!" they shouted. "Over here! There's a woman inside."

Officer Jack and Officer Kate saw a car slowly sinking into the water nose first. The woman inside the car tried to get out, but her door wouldn't open.

"Call it in, Kate!" said Officer Jack. He turned to the crowd. "What happened?" he asked as he took off his belt and radio.

A man spoke up. "She was leaving to go home. When she stepped on the gas her car jumped forward and went over the bank."

"How many are in the car?" he asked as he started down the bank.

"Just one," said a woman.

He heard Officer Kate on the radio.

"Dispatch, this is patrol 14. Over."

"Go ahead, 14," said Dispatch. "Over."

"Requesting ambulance at the Riverfront Park boat ramp. We have a car in the water with a passenger trapped inside. Over."

Officer Kate turned to see Officer Jack pop to the surface. She shouted, "Ambulance is on the way. What's your situation?"

"Doors are locked. Can't get them to open," Officer Jack shouted back. "The car is still sinking."

He dove down again to try a different door.

The woman had climbed into the back seat to get away from the rising water. She looked at Officer Kate through the back window and shouted, "Help me!"

Officer Kate nodded and looked around. She saw a jagged rock the size of a soccer ball.

"Jack!" she shouted as she picked up the rock and headed down the bank. "Use this!"

"Good job, partner," Officer Jack said as he took the rock and raised it over his head.

Officer Kate motioned for the woman to cover her head.

Officer Jack brought the rock down on the window with all his strength. The window shattered.

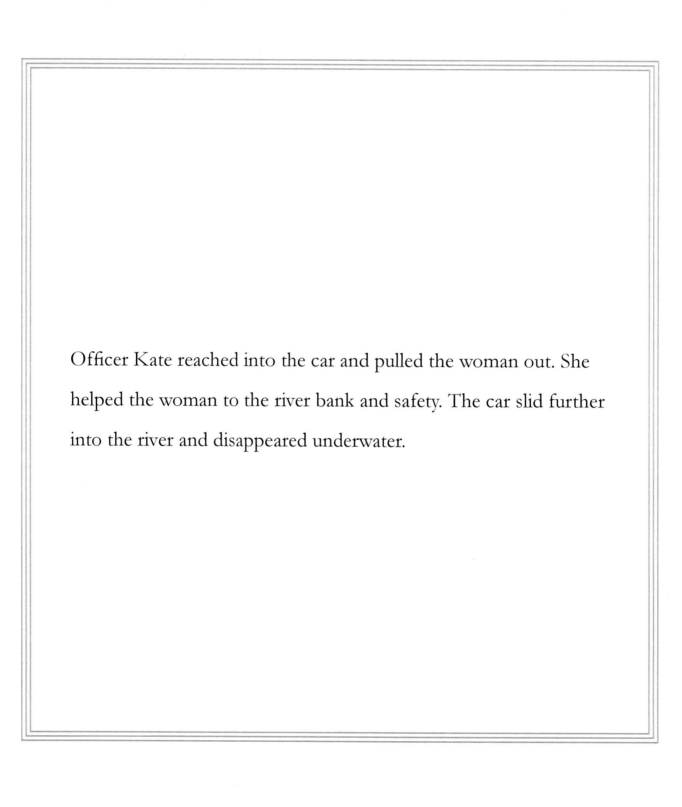

Officer Kate reached into the car and pulled the woman out. She helped the woman to the river bank and safety. The car slid further into the river and disappeared underwater.

EMT Morales came down the bank.

"Officer Jack. Officer Kate," she said, "Still getting yourself into trouble, I see."

"Good to see you too, Morales," said Officer Kate.

EMT Morales continued, "Let's get you and your new friend up to the ambulance and make sure you're all okay."

The woman turned to Officer Jack and Officer Kate.

"Thank you!" she said. "You two saved my life. Thank you!"

Officer Jack thanked God that Officer Kate had noticed the
jagged rock in time to save the woman.

Officer Jack and Officer Kate stood up straight, gave the woman a
quick salute, and said,

"Glad to do it!"

Meet the Author

James (Jim) Burd Brewster is the author of the Uncle Rocky, Fireman series which are now joined with this book by the Officer Jack series. He was raised in Albany, NY, learned to sail on Lake Champlain, navigated a Polar Icebreaker in the US Coast Guard, and married Katie Spivey from Wilmington, NC. His writing career started when he and Katie took a creative writing class as "Empty-Nesters." Professor Wayne Karlin's class gave him the desire to write down the Uncle Rocky, Fireman stories, Christina Allen's advice gave him the confidence to publish them, and Yvonne Medley's Life Journey's Writers Club gave him the technical knowledge to do it. He can be contacted through: www.gladtodoit.net

Meet the Illustrator

Mary Barrows is a freelance illustrator from the small town of Walkersville, MD. Since she was old enough to hold a pencil, she has been drawing pictures of her favorite stories, and she hasn't stopped yet. She is the second oldest of six kids with a passion for children's books and fantasy stories. When she isn't illustrating, Mary loves to read, play basketball, and mess around on her guitar.
She can be contacted through:
www.marybarrowsillustration.com